THE TERRIBLES ARE TERROR-IFIC!

READ ALL THE BOOKS IN THE SERIES!

Welcome to Stubtoe Elementary

A Witch's Last Resort

Clash of the Gnomes!

THE TERRIBLES

WELCOME TO STUBTOE ELEMENTARY

TRAVIS NICHOLS

WITHDRAWN

A YEARLING BOOK

All rights reserved. Published in the United States by Yearling,
an imprint of Random House Children's Books, a division of
Penguin Random House LLC, New York. Originally published in
hardcover in the United States by Random House Children's Books,
a division of Penguin Random House LLC, New York, in 2022.

Yearling and the jumping horse design
are registered trademarks of Penguin Random House LLC.

Visit us on the Web! rhcbooks.com

Educators and librarians, for a variety of teaching tools,
visit us at RHTeachersLibrarians.com

Library of Congress Cataloging-in-Publication Data
is available upon request.
ISBN 978-0-593-42571-8 (hc)—
ISBN 978-0-593-42572-5 (lib. bdg.)—
ISBN 978-0-593-42573-2 (ebook)—
ISBN 978-0-593-42574-9 (pbk.)

Printed in the United States of America
10 9 8 7 6 5 4 3 2 1
First Yearling Edition 2023

To Greyson,

THE MOST DISGUSTING, KINDHEARTED,
TERRIBLEST, PRECIOUS GOBLIN ON EARTH

CONTENTS

VOTE 4
CHORDIN

WELCOME TO CREEP'S COVE

First things first, dear reader. Despite what you might have been told, they're all real. The monsters, the cryptids, the ghosts, the creeps. All of them.

That house a few blocks over that you're *sure* is haunted? You've got great intuition. It's *loaded* with poltergeists. The boogeyman under your bed? She's real, but don't worry about her. She's a vegetarian. Mostly.

Goblins, mummies, swamp creatures, zombies? Yep, yep, yep, yep. Aliens? They're

1

even more bug-eyed-bizarre than you can imagine. Sasquatches, chupacabras, mothmen, Loch Ness monsters? Of course.

There. Now that we've got that squared away—don't freak out. It's not as bad as you think.

Here's the deal. Before you were born, the world was a much different place. For centuries and centuries, monsters roamed freely and fearlessly.

Three-hundred-foot-tall kaijus toppled entire cities. Vampires and werewolves terrorized small villages. Fringe scientists* schemed, and opera house phantoms cut chandeliers loose onto crowds.

---

* A FRINGE SCIENTIST (OR PARA-SCIENTIST) IS SOMEONE WHO STUDIES AND PRACTICES SCIENCE THAT ISN'T ACCEPTED BY THE BROADER COMMUNITY. EXAMPLES INCLUDE CRYPTOZOOLOGY, ASTROLOGY, PARAPSYCHOLOGY, AND COLLAGE.

Their fear-fueled, chaotic reign was unstoppable.

But eventually—and this was just a few years before you came along—*most* of the monsters* of the world decided they needed to settle down.

They packed their stuff and moved to an island called Creep's Cove, waaay out in the middle of the fish-stinking ocean. There they could work regular jobs, pick up hobbies, and raise their families under a volcanic haze of permanent dusk.

So you've got a lot less to worry about than you did a couple of pages ago. Go on with your life. Put this book down and see if there are any chores you should be doing.

What's that? You want to know more about the monstrous residents of Creep's

---

* AND MONSTER-ADJACENT HUMANS

Cove? Are you sure you aren't just trying to get out of doing chores? Great. So. Creep's Cove is, for the most part, a pretty typical community: houses, stores, portals to various nightmarish parallel dimensions, offices, cars, a river of radioactive slime, etc. The residents have normal lives. They mow their lawns, buy groceries, and send their kids to school.

FEBRUSCARY

#1 MUM

THE ROTTEN KIDS OF STUBTOE ELEMENTARY

The first thing that the founders of Creep's Cove built was a bagel shop. Adults love saying things like *It's just so hard to get a good bagel out here.* Knifeteeth Mike's Bagel Wasteland boasted seven kinds of bagels, and they were all terrible. But it wasn't Knifeteeth Mike's fault. See, you gotta have the right water to get a soft, chewy bagel. It's basically impossible to get a good bagel in most places.

Anyway, the second thing the founders

Knifeteeth Mike's Signature Bagels

Almost
Everything

Morning
Mushroom

Nothing

Actual
Poison

Blue Cheese
(not on purpose)

Whatever Was
in That Barrel

built was a school for all the kids being born, spawned, hatched, and summoned on the island. They named it Stubtoe Elementary for no actual reason whatsoever. There's honestly no story there. Let's move on.

There are a few classrooms in Stubtoe Elementary, but only one teacher/principal/custodian/lunch monitor. Ms. Verne is more than capable of handling it all. Ms. Verne . . . sort of came with the island. Some say she came with the planet. At any rate, the kids love her.

Some students have expressed interest in an exchange program, where a few humans could travel to Creep's Cove and spend a semester

← Ms. Verne

Haunted
Wheat

with them, but they haven't figured out a way to guarantee that the visitors wouldn't be eaten immediately, even with scent-blocking cream. Until then, hopefully this book can give you a safe introduction to the students at Stubtoe Elementary.

Let's take a look at you. You're not a whiny little baby. Hmm. But you're also not what anyone would call *mature* by any means. No offense. Anyway, if you were to somehow move to Creep's Cove and enroll in school (and not be battered, fried, and gobbled up like a giant, piping-hot, oozing cheese stick), you'd likely be put in the older-ish class at Stubtoe Elementary. Any older and you'd likely be at the middle school across the field. So—do you want to mostly focus on that group of kids? Perfect. Then it's settled.

GOOD MORNING, VLAD

Vlad had pointy ears, pointy hair, and pointy teeth. He wore a pointy cape and pointy shoes. Vlad was a vampire.

Vampires avoid sunlight, as it tends to make them explode horribly. Fortunately, the volcano at the center of Creep's Cove consistently chugged out a thick curtain of smoke, so Vlad and the other vampires could keep a daytime schedule with everyone else.

Vlad and his parents were watching *The Most Ghosts,* a show about two families of ghosts annoyingly/hilariously haunting the same house, when a news bulletin cut in.

"Attention, all residents of Creep's Cove," announced a handsome pile of goo. "Due to power plant maintenance, local (fringe) scientists will temporarily halt the activity of our

central volcano. From ten a.m. to eleven a.m. tomorrow, smoke will cease to spew, ash will cease to fall, and magma will cease to flow. In that hour, the (gulp) *sun* will peek through and shine upon our fair island. All vampires, wraiths, and other photosensitive beings should shut themselves away from the loathsome, insidious sun during that time. Furthermore, werewolves, weretigers, werekoalas (*aaawww!*), and anyone who would devolve to their delicious human form under its direct rays should make sure to apply scent-blocking cream. Okay, bye."

Vlad's mom snapped her fingers. The TV went dark. "Well, you'll be staying home from school tomorrow."

"What? Aw, come on," pleaded Vlad. "I wanna see it."

"You cannot," said Vlad's mom. "You would explode horribly."

"I'll just take a little bitty peek."

"You'd explode," said Vlad's father, with emphasis. "Horribly."

Vlad turned into six bats and stormed off to his room.

Later, Vlad's father knocked on his door. Vlad waved his hand, and the door whooshed open.

"May I come in?"

"Yes. You may enter."*

_____

* VAMPIRES CAN'T ENTER YOUR HOME WITHOUT AN INVITATION. VAMPIRE PARENTS PRACTICE THIS RULE WITH THEIR KIDS. THEY ALSO PRACTICE AVOIDING WOODEN STAKES.

Vlad's father glided in through the door-
way on his tiptoes in that cool vampire way
and hovered near the edge of the coffin.
"My son, I have just spoken to Ms. Verne.
She assures me that you and other children
in danger of the sun—one million curses
upon it—will be tucked away in the cloak
closet when it comes out. You can go to
school if you promise to be safe."

"Of course, Father. I have a plan."

"You have a what?"

"I . . . have a plan . . . to be safe. I plan to be safe."

Everyone at school the next morning was buzzing about the sunlight.

"I hear it's like a big ball of glowing goo," glurfed Bobby, a gelatinous glob.

"That's pretty close, actually," replied Frankie, a (fringe) scientist and all-around

know-it-all. "It's a flaming ball of gas. About seventy percent hydrogen, twenty-eight percent helium, and—"

"I'll smash it to pieces if it gets near me!" yelled Lizzie, a reptilian kaiju with, as you can already tell, a bit of an anger management problem.

At 9:45, Ms. Verne slapped a tentacle on her desk. "Δˈʃˆ¥°Δ≤˜μʃ†◊ø."

"Yes, Ms. Verne," said Quade, the nicest kid in class.* He opened the cloak closet door and read from the list on the chalkboard. "Vlad (would explode), Emma, Lobo. Here you go."

Vlad sulked, Emma trudged, and Lobo trotted to the cloak closet. Quade shut it behind them and locked it.

---

* AND NOT JUST NICE FOR A SASQUATCH, WHO ARE FAMOUSLY NICE, AS YOU KNOW

"∞'↑§∞ ´•° ¬°∆Å•," said Ms. Verne.

"YOU HEARD THE LADY. MOVE OUT!" shouted Lizzie.

As the rest of the class went outside, Lobo pulled a blanket out of a basket and laid it on the floor. He walked in eight or nine circles on it* and then plopped down.

"Well, I had *no* interest in spending a couple of hours as a human, and obviously Vlad can't go out, but why are you here, Emma? Mummies aren't photo-whatchamacallit."

Emma pointed to an exposed section of pickled flesh sticking out from the wrappings on her arm. "RRROT."

Lobo sniffed at the air and nodded. "Ah. Gross."

There was a clicking sound from outside the door.

"Well," said Vlad, "I'll be going now."

---

* ALL WEREWOLVES DO THIS—IT'S PRETTY ADORABLE.

18

"What are you doing?" asked Lobo.

The door opened, and Bobby pluffed proudly on the other side. He was still smamming the key-shaped glob of an appendage he had used to plarf the lock. He glorped it back into his body.

"Shall we?"

Vlad nodded and ran toward Bobby. He leapt into the air and executed a perfect swan dive right into Bobby's belly.

Bobby splarged out, shlarfing Vlad completely.

"To the playground!" shouted Vlad, his voice muffled in the ooze.

Bobby/Vlad diffled the closet door and mubbled out of the classroom.

Everyone, including the annoying babies in the younger class and the supercool older kids from the middle school across the field, were out on the playground. Bobby/Vlad sneebled over near the rest of their class and gloofed* behind a dead tree. Just then, the haze overhead got thinner . . . and thinner . . . and gave way to a blue sky. Beams of sunlight poured over the students. They screamed in terror. They cheered. They danced in it. They shouted and shook their fists at it. Erik, the

---

* BY THE WAY, THERE'S A COMPLETE GLOSSARY OF BOBBY'S VERBS AT THE END OF THE BOOK, IF YOU NEED HELP YORBLING ANYTHING.

gloomiest songwriting (human) phantom on Creep's Cove, whistled a tune that could almost be considered cheerful.

"Well?" gorgled Bobby.

"Juuuuust a little bit," said Vlad. "Let's be certain." Bobby/Vlad leebled out and toobled an arm into the sunbeam. It felt warm, but there were no explosions. Not even smoke.

"Bobby, I am a *genius,*" said Vlad. "Let's bask."

Bobby/Vlad lorfed out from the tree's shade and glopped over to Lizzie and Quade. "Vlad?! Is that you in there?!" exclaimed Lizzie.

"Sssssshhh! Sure is, friends. So . . . this is the sun."

"Apparently so," said Quade. "I like it."

"Not me!" yelled Lizzie. "It hurts when I stare at it."

"**¬ძ°ΔΛ̈ÉΔ°˙¬ȿ⊙̂ÜΔ,**" called Ms. Verne.

"Right right right. Don't look directly at it. I forgot."

"So . . . how much less pink is it than what I'm seeing?" asked Vlad.

"It's not pink at all," said Frankie, poking at Bobby. "This gelatinous coating—great idea, by the way—is completely obscuring your view. However, were it sunrise, the sun would be passing through more atmosphere—and thus more molecules—scattering the wavelengths of light and making for a wider assortment of colors—pinks, oranges, reds, purples. . . ."

"Excuse me, Frankie, but this is supposed to be a *break* from learning," said Lizzie. At *break,* she punted a ball over the horizon.

"I'm glad you shared that, Frankie," said Quade. "Thanks."

The class played for another forty minutes
or so. Then there was a *POP* from the center of the island, and the volcano resumed
chugging smoke. Ms. Verne called everyone
inside.

Bobby/Vlad dorbled ahead of the group.
Once inside, Vlad florbed out of Bobby and
tucked himself back in the cloak closet.

"How was it?" asked Lobo.

"Sticky."

The rest of the class filtered in, and Quade
opened the closet door. Vlad stepped out,

whistling an innocent tune. Emma and Lobo took their seats.

Vlad scratched his head in mock puzzlement as he sat down. "So, let me get this straight. You can go out in it, but you can't look at it, and if you're out in it too long, you can get burned by it? Meh. I guess I didn't miss anything."

One of Ms. Verne's tentacles raced over to Vlad and grabbed him out of his seat. It squeezed. Vlad hissed. Another tentacle shot over, plucked something from his hair, and whipped it toward Bobby. Bobby was

kloffed out of his chair by the flying chunk of goo, which had been overlooked when Vlad and Bobby separated. Bobby reflurfed his missing glob. Ms. Verne dropped Vlad back into his seat.

At lunch, Bobby durfed over to Vlad. "By the way, the Hendersons baked a new cake to replace the one the Smiths destroyed."

"What are you talking about?"

"*The Most Ghosts* episode you didn't finish last night. You were wondering how it ended."

Vlad sighed. "Bobby, please don't absorb my thoughts if we do that again."

"I just took a little bitty peek."

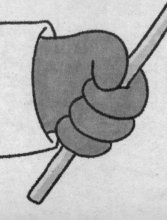

Frankie presents...
SCIENCE CHUNKS

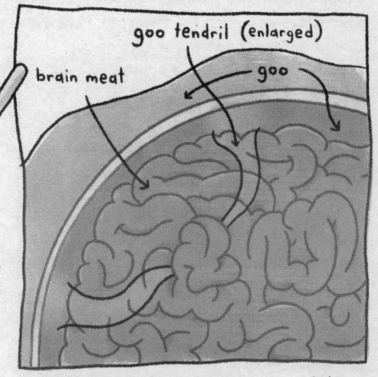

Fig 1. How a gelatinous glob can absorb your thoughts

Register with the MORTAL AFFAIRS OFFICE.
All visitors and new residents must check
in and apply for entry with one of our
friendly MORTAL AFFAIRS representatives.

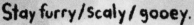
Stay furry/scaly/gooey.
It is highly suggested that shape-shifters avoid their human forms if possible.

Get involved!
The MORTAL AFFAIRS OFFICE houses a wide
selection of flyers and social calendars.

FRANKIE MAKES
A FRIEND

Frankie was an only child with an only dad. As one of the founders of Creep's Cove, Dr. Shelley had transformed the volcano at the center of the island into a sun-blocking power source. He was a very important human being, and the residents of the island rewarded him by not ripping him and his daughter into a dozen pieces and eating them. To be extra safe, he also invented the scent-blocking cream that the handful of humans on the island slathered on their skin suits every day.

Frankie loved to sit on a countertop in her dad's lab and watch him work. He did all sorts of experiments. He turned mud into gold and gold into delicious tomato soup. He zapped plants with various rays until they sprouted legs and danced around the room. It was very important work, and Frankie was determined to follow in his footsteps.

One morning, Frankie skipped into her dad's lab and found him lowering a rope into the trash portal. "What are you working on, Dad?"

"Ah, Frankie. I've been throwing our garbage into this worm-

hole for a few weeks now, and I decided I should discover where in the universe it's going. I attached a rope to a camera, and I'm getting some footage."

"Can I help?"

"I've got it under control, Critter, but if you're feeling science-y,

why don't you see what you can find in my spare-parts bins?"

Frankie leapt off the counter and ran for the garage. Having free rein of the spare-parts bins was a rare treat.

The crates in the garage were stacked ten high and labeled with duct tape: BEAKERS AND BOTTLES, WIRES (ASSORTED), ARMS/LEGS, MOLDS, FUNGI, HEADS/HEAD STUFF, ACCESSO-RIES, LOOSE TOES, TORSOS, ODDS AND ENDS.

Frankie loaded stuff into a wheelbarrow and hauled it to her lab. She ███ bones ███ face. Her chain saw was a little rusty, but she managed to ████ ████ ████. "Now . . . where's that blowtorch? Ah, yes." ██ █████ ██ ██. The hardest part was ██ █ the ████ █████, but some stitching and staples ███ ██. With her hammer, Frankie ███ ██ ████ with ██ █████ ███.*

Frankie wheeled a sheet-covered gurney into her dad's lab. Dr. Shelley was leaning back in his chair, watching a monitor. On the screen, a group of hairy lizards squirmed around in a pile of garbage.

---

* AAARG, THE ALLIANCE OF ADULTS AGAINST RAMPANT GROSSNESS, HAS DETERMINED THAT THE DETAILED DESCRIPTION OF FRANKIE SEWING, HAMMERING, AND MELTING BODY PARTS TOGETHER IS FAR TOO GORY AND DISGUSTING TO INCLUDE IN THIS BOOK, SO YOU'LL HAVE TO IMAGINE IT. IMAGINE IT. NO, IT'S GROSSER. GROSSER THAN THAT. EVEN GROSSER. THERE. YOU GOT IT.

"Check it out, Critter. Found out where the wormhole goes," said Dr. Shelley.

"Yikes! I guess you'll have to find a new place to dump our trash."

"No—they love it." Just then, a plump lizard slithered into view, wearing a crown of empty cans. The other creatures wiggled at the sight of their queen and presented her with a selection of used napkins.

"Dad?" asked Frankie. "Can you help me finish my project?"

Dr. Shelley turned away from the monitor. "Ah! What did you make?"

"I made a new friend."

The body was made up of parts from a few different people. The arms didn't match, and the head was a bit of a mash-up. At the sum of its parts, it looked like a boy about the same age as Frankie.

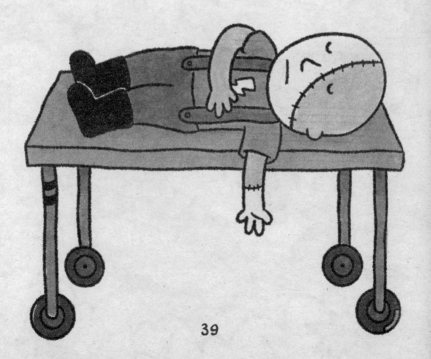

Frankie attached wired suction cups to the body's face and heart. Dr. Shelley cranked open the skylight and flipped a bunch of very science-y switches. A copper antenna creaked out above the lab and up into the sky. A rumble of thunder seemed to call out a warning. Almost immediately, a bolt of lightning struck the antenna and raced down to the machinery below.

The body on the gurney flailed wildly as electricity coursed through its bones and mushy bits. Then . . . it was quiet. Dr. Shelley lowered the antenna and closed the skylight.

Frankie popped off the suction cups and looked directly into the face of a living boy. His eyes (one green and one brown) blinked independently at different speeds.*

"Are you my mom?"

Frankie was shocked. "Oh. That wasn't . . . really my intention. I'm Frankie."

"I'm . . ." The boy was confused. "I'm a little of this and a little of that, I think."

"You'll figure it out in time. For now, let's call you Adam."

Dr. Shelley clapped Frankie and Adam on their backs. "Great. You kids go have fun. I'm going to see what happens when I throw a

---

* DOES THAT TECHNICALLY MAKE IT WINKING?

bunch of hot sauce into the wormhole. Ah, yes, there is nothing more important than the pursuit of scientific discovery, as well as following one's great passions in life. Remember that."

After a brief quiz, Ms. Verne placed Adam in the little kids' class at school. Frankie had been looking forward to being in class

with her new friend,* but she knew they'd still have plenty of time after school and on weekends to play.

At lunch, Frankie went over to the little kids' section of the cafeteria to say hi to Adam.

"BIG KID ALERT!" shouted an annoying little ghoul.

* ... OR SON? WAIT, YEAH, THAT'S WEIRD.

"Everybody, act cool!" whispered a snot-faced goblin.

"Heya, Frankie," said Adam.

"You *know* her?" asked an irritating ghost.

"Walk with me," said Adam.

Adam picked up his lunch tray and carried it over to the window to the kitchen. A tentacle reached out and grabbed it from his hands.

"Hey, thanks, Ms. V."

"So," asked Frankie, "how are you liking school?"

"Oh, it's great," said Adam. "I'm learning a lot. We're doing shapes. Did you know there's like *three* different shapes? See, first, there's circles. Then you got your squareses. Then, outta nowhere, boom, *triangles*."

"I'm glad you're enjoying it. So, after school I thought we could—"

"Yeah, I wanted to talk to you about that,"

interrupted Adam. "Listen, I'm really glad you brought me to life and all, and school is great, but part of me wants to . . . work. To pull my weight around the house, y'know?"

"Well, I have a few chores that we could split," offered Frankie.

"No, like *work*. There's a big chunk of me that used to work a bulldozer at a scrapyard. I must've griped about that job a hundred and fifty billion times back then, but I see now that I got a lot out of using my hands and working hard, y'know?"

"I don't know about that even a little bit," replied Frankie. "But I'll do whatever I can to help."

"Thanks, Frankie," said Adam. "You're a great mom. And a great friend."

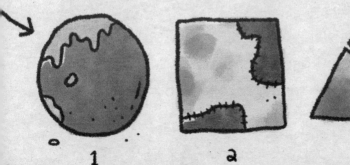

1   2   3

After school, Frankie and Adam went down to the wharf. Adam stepped into the harbor-master's office, and five minutes later, he came out with a little knit hat and a part-time job as a dockworker.

"They got me coming in on evenings and weekends," said Adam. "Look at me. Learning about shapes. New job. Big day for Adam."

The harbormaster leaned out of her office and bellowed for Adam to unload a nearby fishing boat. He gave a salute to his boss. Then to Frankie, he shouted, "See ya at home, Mom!" before running down the dock.

Frankie knew she wouldn't be seeing as much of Adam as she'd like. Being an adult—or even one-third adult—means being busy, busy, busy. She watched Adam drag a crate from the rusted boat. "Hey, Adam," she yelled, pointing at the side of the box. "See that? *Rectangle*."

Adam dropped the crate and stared at it in disbelief. "They got *four* shapes? This day is unreal!"

GILLY MAKES A MESS

Young Gilly's home was in a swamp
Where serpents hiss and gators chomp.

Her mother reigned beneath the mire
And hoped that Gilly would aspire

To one day don the Crown of Night
And take the throne as her birthright.

But this gave Gilly much distress,
For this great Queendom was a mess.

Since chaos was the rule of law,

The Queen was angry when she saw …

That Gilly kept her bog quite clean.

Her muck in stacks: brown, yellow, green.

The bugs were sorted by last names.
The moss was trimmed on Saturdays.

The slime was swept; the mud was mopped;
The mushrooms all had polished tops.

The Queen asked Gilly in her lair,
"My daughter–do ye even care?"

"What ye've done here is a disgrace!
'Tis not the nature of this place."

"I lead in bedlam! Disarray!
I be quite shocked at this display."

"If ye must tidy your cesspool,
Then ye are not equipped to rule."

"But, Mother, never have I said
I sought to be our Queendom's head."

"I know not yet what I might do.
Can I be me and ye be you?"

"Forgive me, child, I did not know.

I never asked if ye felt so."

"Fret not, my child, for do recall,

I am immortal, after all."

TERRIBLE TOPICS:

TELL US ABOUT YOUR

ROOM

Is it still a bedroom...

...if I can't find the bed?

THAAAT'S MEEE.

THAAAT'S MMMEEE.

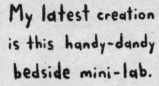
My latest creation is this handy-dandy bedside mini-lab.

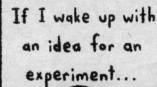
If I wake up with an idea for an experiment...

BOOM!

Science.

My den be my sanctuary within the madness.

Please wipe your feet.

I fill the darkness with song, and I fill my songs... with darkness.

Maybe I should just get a lamp.

Nothing beats that fresh pine smell. Mmm.

Breathe it in.

THAAAT'S-

THAAAT'S PICKLES.

LOBO GETS GROOMED

L obo was little. He was the littlest kid in his class, had a little voice, and was a little itchy most of the time.

When he scratched an itch in class, some-one would say *Hey, what time is it?* and someone else would answer *It's scratch-thirty.* At some point, it was updated to *itch scratch-thirty,* then *itch scratch-hurty.* Gilly tried out *'tis the itching hour,* but it didn't stick. What is it about teasing that inspires so much creativity?

So Lobo was beyond excited when he saw Emma scratching her neck one morning. He called out, "Hey, anybody know what time it is?"

Lizzie pointed at the clock with a foreleg. "It's nine-fifteen."

"No," said Lobo. "Look at Emma. What time is it?"

"Well, now it's nine-sixteen. Ms. Verne, Lobo needs a clock-reading refresher."

"Forget it," said Lobo.

Later, during an Ancient Curses lesson,

Quade began to squirm in his seat. Then Frankie and Erik started scratching their arms and legs. Vlad hissed, jumped up, and grabbed the ceiling. Gilly slapped her shoulders and face. Lizzie shouted, **"YEEEEEOOOW!"** and flipped her desk.

Ms. Verne lifted Lizzie up with one tentacle and grabbed at her tail with another. ¨Ȯȃ¯ı◊π.¨

"Fleas? **FLEAS?!**" Lizzie thrashed around until Ms. Verne dropped her. She looked around the room. Every single student was scratching and writing around. "It's a full-blown infestation!"

Frankie rushed to the front of the room. She drew a bunch of squares on the chalkboard and marked each one with a capital letter. She paused to scratch her armpit, then pointed at a square on the edge of the chart marked *Li.* "Okay—Lizzie most recently got

itchy." Frankie drew an arrow from the *Li* to the *G*. "Before that was Gilly . . . and Vlad. Before that, we have Erik and me. . . ."

It took about six seconds to determine that Lobo was Patient Zero: the center of the flea outbreak. He was sent home with a note.

Lobo, his parents, and his older sister spent a lovely afternoon together at the groomer. It started with soothing hot-spring flea dips, followed by head-to-toe fur trims. Then they got manicures and pedicures. When it was time to choose a nail polish color, Lobo couldn't decide between Forgotten Leftovers and Soggy Driftwood. The zombie nail tech leaned forward and whispered, "They're both just brown, kid."

Lobo wasn't itchy at all, which made him realize just how itchy he was before. It felt

nice. It felt . . . quiet. With his clear, non-itchy mind, his senses kicked in. He smelled the rancid stew that one of the workers was eating in the back room. He heard bats clicking and fluttering outside. He suddenly remembered where he left his favorite squeaky ball three months earlier.

Finally, he was led to a desk where his clothes were neatly folded. They had been washed and stitched up. He changed out of his fluffy robe and into his new-old T-shirt and shorts.

Walking back to the car, the family of werewolves looked like gazillionaire movie stars. A group of goblins was putting the final touches on the family's station wagon. Lobo's mom tipped each of the goblins with a little chunk of gold and took the keys.

The werewolves drove home, all with

their furry heads leaning out the windows
and tongues lolling in the smoggy breeze.

As they pulled into the driveway, exterminators were removing a tarp from the house. A werefrog in a jumpsuit handed Lobo's mom a clipboard. "You're all set. Every last flea, tick, roach, louse, and ant has been gassed and collected in this bucket."

Lobo's mom signed the form and handed the clipboard back to the werefrog.

The werefrog smiled. "Yep. No bugs in the house at all. Got 'em all."

"Thank you so much," said Lobo's dad.

"Our pleasure." The werefrog cleared his throat.

Lobo's parents looked at each other.

The werefrog shuffled his feet and looked nervously at the bucket. "So, um . . . can we . . ."

"Yes, you can keep the bugs."

The werefrog exterminators all cheered in unison.

When Lobo showed up at school the next morning, his hair was big and puffy, his clothes were crisp and clean, and his claws were trimmed and painted. His classmates were quiet when they saw him. Vlad was the first to speak. He pointed at Lobo's claws. "Forgotten Leftovers? Nice choice."

With that comment, the tension in the room was lifted. "I'm sorry I called you out yesterday," said Frankie. "It was for science."

"That's okay," said Lobo. "I feel a lot better now."

"HAIR BIIIIG," groaned Emma.

"Thanks," said Lobo.

"We all had to take flea medicine because of you," grumbled Lizzie. "It was *disgusting*."

"I'm sorry," said Lobo.

At recess, Quade found Lobo leaned up against a tree. "Are you okay?" he asked.

"I guess so," said Lobo. "I just feel very . . . vivid."

"I had a feeling." Quade handed Lobo a pair of scissors.

With a few snips at his clothes and a little

roll in the dirt, Lobo felt a lot more like himself. Back at his desk, he absentmindedly scratched at some dirt on his arm. .

Gilly pointed and exclaimed, "What time be it?"

Lizzie jumped out of her seat, shouted **"NOT AGAIN!,"** smashed a Lizzie-shaped hole in the wall, and ran all the way home.

How to Write a Perfect Song

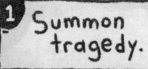

1 Summon tragedy.

2 Conjure the weight of the world.

3 Stare into the abyss.

4 Let it all wash over you.

by ERIK

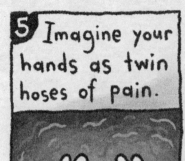

5 Imagine your hands as twin hoses of pain.

6 Turn on the faucets.

7 Pour... pour... POOOOUR!!!

I'll call this one "Rats Stole My Chips."

79

ALLIE'S INVASION

There was an intricate design drawn in the sandbox one morning before school. Swooping circles and lines, shapes crossing one another, and strange symbols—all perfectly etched in the dirt.

"What do you think it means?" asked Quade.

"Maybe it's a maze," offered Lobo.

"Maybe it's just a doodle," gurfled Bobby.

"Mayhaps the wind hath shapeth it," sayeth Gilly.

"*Maybe* it wrecked my T.U.F.F. Squad™ cemetery," growled Lizzie, jumping into the sandbox. Lizzie furiously dug around in the sand and retrieved her buried action figures. "Live! Live again, Centaur-inox 5000! Back to life, Dino Rusty! Welcome back, Gretchen!"

"Okay . . . ," said Vlad. "So much for that cool drawing."

A horrific scream bellowed from the school. The kids traced it to the cloak closet in the little kids' classroom. They opened the door and found the source of the wailing: a fuzzy, boogery hobgoblin.

"What's wrong?" asked Frankie.

"Mrs. Slurp is GONE!" cried the gross little kid.

"Who's Mrs. Slurp?" asked Frankie.

"My favorite. My favorite friend." The hobgoblin was cradling something in her arms. She held it out to Frankie—a purple plush claw.

"Mrs. Slurp is a stuffed animal? Aw, we'll help you find . . . the rest of her."

"I, er, found her, Frankie," said Adam (who had learned not to call Frankie "Mom" in front of the other kids). "And then some." Adam pulled back a row of cloaks, revealing an elaborate pattern of white stuffing. Crisscrossed lines and a perfect spiral of poly-cotton fluff were taped to the wall.

Then they saw it—a pile of stuffless stuffed animal pieces on the ground be-

neath the pattern. **"LOOK AWAAAY!"** jorgled Bobby, skwibbling himself out to block the carnage from the little kids. Frankie and Quade peeled the fluff from the wall and placed it, along with the stuffed animal parts, in a bag. Quade patted the crying kid on the top of her greasy head and took the bag of fluff and stuff back to his classroom.

It was hard for anyone to pay attention to Ms. Verne's slime-mold lesson that morning. All anyone could think about were the strange patterns in the sand and the toy dissection in the little kids' room. When it started raining outside, the kids could barely contain themselves. They were wild. Batty, even. Ms. Verne put away the slime mold and wrote **BOOK TIME OR ELSE** on the board. She smacked the words with a tentacle to show that she meant business. Everyone grabbed something from the book nook and huddled in various corners to whisper their theories.

"I'm telling you—they're mazes," mumbled Lobo. "I almost got to the end before Lizzie wrecked it."

"Perchance," muttered Gilly. "But then what say ye about the toys? They were gutted and strewn about, says I."

"That's why I'm sure it was the wind," murmured Erik. "She's a fierce one, the wind. A trickster. Harsh and unstoppable."

When the rain let up after lunch, everyone went outside for recess. Gilly went straight to the sandbox because that's where the best post-rain worms could be found.

"GASP, I SAY! VERILY!"

Everyone rushed over. There was a new design drawn in the sand—a perfect cube with dotted lines shooting out in every direction.

"Look!" shouted Erik. "Footprints!"

Sure enough, there were little muddy prints from the sandbox leading back to the school.

Lizzie pounded her goofy little forelegs together. "Let's get the sucker!"

The group followed the trail back into the building, down the hall, and to the little kids' classroom. Lobo sniffed at the mud on the floor and pointed at the remaining footprints ahead of them. "They went this way."

"Yeah, we know," blurfed Bobby. "But . . . good job."

There was a ripping sound coming from behind the cloak closet door.

"We should get Ms. Verne," said Quade.

"Not this time," snarled Vlad. "I'll handle this."

Vlad opened the door a couple of inches, looked inside, gave a little *eep!*, turned into four rats, and scuttled down the hall.

Lizzie grabbed the door and threw it

open. There, in the middle of the cloak
closet, stood a bug-eyed creature with a
visible, pulsating brain under a glass dome.

They held half of a plush slug in one hand and a trail of stuffing in the other.

"AHAAAAA!" roared Lizzie. "Now you're gonna get it!"

A tentacle shot out of nowhere and grabbed the intruder. A second one shooed everyone back to class.

"An *alien*," said Lobo.

"Very cool," porfed Bobby. "I wonder if they're from the same place as my mom. I'd love to absorb some old-world cuisine, whatever that is."

"It kinda seems like they're into stuffed animals," said Vlad.

"Well," glurmed Bobby. "I'll eat anything twice. I'll report back."

"Can't wait," said Vlad.

The door to the classroom opened, and the alien stepped through. Everyone held their breath. The alien spoke. "Begin. Transmission . . . This.Being.Is.Designated.

Allie . . . This.Being.Expresses.Regret.For.
The.Actions.Of.This.Being . . . This.Being.Has.
Been.Reassigned.To.This.Sector.For.More.
Advanced.Education . . . End.Transmission."*

"Å"–°„ꭲlí"îÔˇ," said Ms. Verne.

"Begin.Transmission . . . Acknowledged . . .
End.Transmission."

(The Being Designated as) Allie marched
to an empty desk, but she paused next
to it. "Begin.Transmission . . . This.Desk.
Is.Occupied . . . End.Transmission."

"You . . . you can see me?" asked the
empty desk.

Frankie stood up, took a few cautious
steps toward the empty desk, and poked at
the air above the chair. She felt her finger
jab at something headlike.

---

* RECOMMENDATION: WHEN READING ALLIE'S WORDS ALOUD, PINCH YOUR
NOSE SHUT AND SPEAK AS QUICKLY AS POSSIBLE. WHEN READING HER
WORDS SILENTLY IN YOUR HEAD, GO AHEAD AND PINCH YOUR NOSE ANYWAY.

"HEY!" said the nothingness.

"I'm sorry, but is someone there?" asked Frankie.

"Y-yes. It's me . . . Griff," said somebody/nobody.

"Who the heck is Griff?" demanded Lizzie. **"SHOW YOURSELF!"**

"I've . . . been here all year."

"Why haven't you ever said anything?" asked Frankie.

Griff shrugged. Nobody saw.

Vlad pulled a pair of sunglasses out of his desk. He passed them to Frankie, who held them out to the empty space next to her. The sunglasses hung in the air for a second, shifted, then settled. There he was.

"√˜µç˜ç≈ç∂œΣ´®," said Ms. Verne.

Allie moved to another empty desk.

"¶ª©°∆˙∂ . . . ª•ç§ i≤µ≥ ¬Åíı˜," said Ms. Verne.

"That's okay, Ms. Verne," said Griff. "I didn't see me there, either."

LIZZIE'S TEMPER

Our city is looking amazing!

Let's take a snack break.

No NO **NO!**

This skyscraper isn't tall enough!

CRUNCH!

YEEEEFFOW!

Wait.

GRIFF WINS
THE GAME

Griff had nothing-colored eyes and nothing-colored hair. He wasn't a fan of his knobby nose, but it didn't bother him too much, because nobody could see it. Not even Griff. The only thing anyone ever saw of Griff was the pair of sunglasses he wore so they'd know where he was and could look at him while talking to him (and not stomp on his bare toes).

Hey, stop giggling. Yes, Griff was in the buff. He wore his birthday suit. He was nude.

Au naturel. He walked around naked, okay? Can we move on now?

Griff had just finished working through a book titled *The Cure for Shyness: Learn to Let Your Light Shine with Self-Guided Hypnosis, Practice with Puppets, and Cool Catchphrases.* Before Ms. Verne lent him the book, Griff had managed to speak only twenty-five words to his classmates. Now, with the successful closing of the final chapter of *The Cure for Shyness,* Griff was ready to begin a new chapter . . . in his life.

It would all start with a "Satur-hang with his chumarinos." That was one of the cool catchphrases that Griff was trying out. He wasn't sure the catchphrase itself would become "a thing," but that didn't matter as much as the invitation he had received from Lobo to come over for snacks and games.

Griff loved games. Specifically, he loved hide-and-seek. He had never been found a single time in any game he'd ever played. Of course, *before*, nobody else knew he was playing. But this time was different. This was his chance to dominate hide-and-seek—with other kids actually knowing he was there.

As soon as Lobo's front door shut behind him, Griff yelled, **"HI LOBO OH HI GILLY LET'S PLAY HIDE-AND-SEEK GILLY IS IT!"**

Then he put his sunglasses down on the piano bench and ran down the hall.

"Indeed," said Gilly. She covered her eyes, turned toward the banister at the foot of the stairs, and began to count.

Griff stood behind a drape in the dining room.

From the front of the house, Gilly shouted, "BE YE READY OR NOT, HERE COMETH GILLY." Griff heard doors slamming, drawers opening, and floorboards creaking.

Quiet and still—I am one with the drape, Griff thought.

Suddenly, Gilly threw the drape aside and stared right through Griff before turning and running out of the room. "Come out, come out, wherever ye beee!"

Griff didn't move. Between the beats of his pounding heart, he heard action two doors down. "Found ye, Lobo! I heardeth ye panting and scratching from a mile away!" That

was Griff's cue. He bolted out of the dining room and ran for home base. He knocked over a tall stack of newspapers as he dashed by.

Gilly and Lobo ran into the room. "Where . . . are you, Griff?"

"Oh yeah," said Griff, taking his sunglasses from the piano bench and placing them on his face. "I'm right here at home base."

"Verily," said Gilly. "That means ye be It, Lobo."

"Sounds goooo-ooood," howled Lobo. He turned to the banister and began to count. "One . . . two . . . three . . ."

And Griff was down the hall again, his sunglasses clattering on the floor next to the piano.

Griff wasn't found for seven more rounds. He hid under beds, behind coatracks, in cupboards. In one round, he simply sat in the kitchen eating some terrible-tasting bone-shaped cookies with a cute puppy on the box. Gilly ran right by him. He was the hide-

and-seek *champion,* but it wasn't super fun anymore.

At his eighth *Olly olly oxen free,** Gilly and Lobo sulked into the room. "Can we play something else now?" asked Lobo. "You're too good at hiding, Griff."

Griff was just as bored and defeated as his friends, but they didn't know it. It's hard to notice a look of disappointment on an invisible boy. It's hard to notice anything—messy hair, a knobby nose, hunched shoulders. . . .

Griff had an idea.

"Just one more round. You're It, Gilly. You too, Lobo. You're *both* It, okay?"

"I supposeth," said Gilly.

Lobo and Gilly covered their eyes and began to count. Griff ran straight for the bathroom and opened the medicine cabinet.

---

* BELIEVE IT OR NOT, THIS NONSENSICAL PHRASE WAS CREATED BY HUMAN BEINGS.

Now, it's pretty rude to go through the medicine cabinet at a friend's house. You definitely shouldn't do it. It's only warranted under two circumstances: (1) getting some mouthwash after accidentally eating dog biscuits or (2) salvaging a friendship. This time it was both. After a quick rinse to get the nasty cookie taste out, Griff grabbed a big tube of toothpaste and stepped into the bathtub, pulling the curtain shut behind him.

Griff took off the tube's cap and squeezed the toothpaste into his nothing-colored palms. It was bright pink and smelled like bubble gum. He closed his nothing-colored eyes and smeared the goo all over his head, shoulders, and arms.

Quiet and still. I am one with the bathtub.

Lobo and Gilly slowly crept into the bath-room.

"Oh, Griiiii–iiiiiff?" called Gilly. "He be not in the laundry hamper. Mayhaps."

Griff squeezed his eyes shut even tighter.

"Where aaaaaare you?" sang Lobo. "He's not under the sink . . . I don't think."

Griff put his hands over his mouth.

The shower curtain whooooshed open. **"YAAAAA!!!"** screamed Lobo. "Oh! Griff!"

"We found ye!" called Gilly. "Hey, nice nose."

Griff sneezed. "Okay! What do you want to play next?"

"Let's keep playing hide-and-seek," said Lobo.

"Yeah, ye be It, chumarino."

And as he tracked pink footprints all over Lobo's house, Griff decided that seeking can be even more fun than hiding.

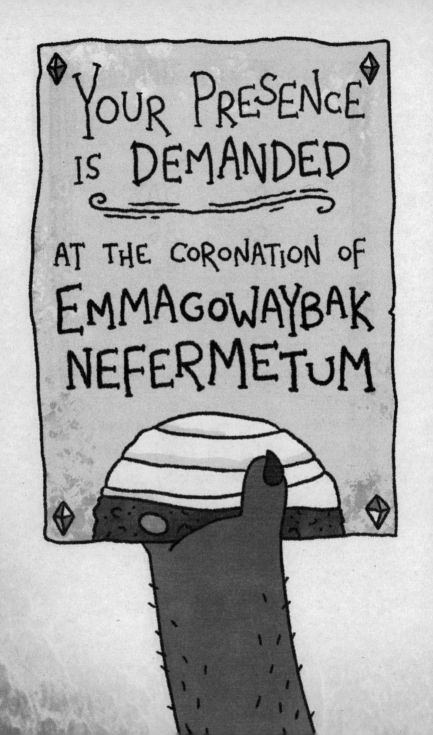

ERIK'S SONG

Erik had deep, oozing scars covering half his face. That's what he'd tell you if you asked, but you'd just have to trust him. He kept the gore covered by a mask at all times. He'd also tell you that the intense sadness he felt about his horrifying face was the source of his one true passion: music. Erik spent hours alone in his attic writing the most miserable songs you could ever imagine. He kept his music private but knew that one day he'd unleash his masterpieces on the world. Then they'd know. They'd aaaaall know.

"Good news," said Vlad, clapping Erik and Allie on the back. "I got us a gig."

"What are you talking about?" asked Erik.

"Emma's birthday party this weekend. Her coronation. She said our band could play it."

"What band?"

"Remember?" said Vlad. "A couple days ago, the three of us were throwing little rocks at that big rock—"

"Oh, that was so fun."

"Yeah, and you muttered, *Maybe I should start a band.*"

Erik tapped his chin thoughtfully. "I suppose . . . maybe I said that? Allie?"

"Begin.Transmission . . . The.Being.Known. As.Erik.Said.Maybe.I.Should.Start.A.Band . . . Then.This.Being.Struck.The.Large.Rock. With.A.Small.Rock . . . End.Transmission."

"Boom," said Vlad.

"Oh. I guess this is how bands are formed," said Erik.

"Yep—this is how it happens,"* said Vlad. "So we should practice. After school?"

Allie bowed. "Begin.Transmission . . . This. Being.Acknowledges—"

Erik's future unfolded before him. This was it. The world would be plunged into the sorrowful depths of his genius. "Go home, grab whatever instruments you have, and come to my house. This is gonna be *forte.*" Erik pounded an air keyboard and ran toward home. **"FORTE!"**

"I have no idea what 'for-tay' is,"† said Vlad. "But I gotta say—I *love* the enthusiasm."

---

* THIS IS EXACTLY HOW BANDS ARE FORMED. BY THE WAY, YOU SHOULD START A BAND.

† FORTE, IN MUSIC, MEANS LOUD. IT ALSO MEANS SOMETHING YOU'RE GOOD AT. FOR EXAMPLE, EATING SO MUCH SPAGHETTI IS BOBBY'S FORTE.

Vlad wheeled a giant suitcase into Erik's garage. He laid it flat and unzipped it but didn't open it.

"Ooh, what did you bring?" asked Erik. "Drums? Trombone? Banjo?"

"Better," said Vlad. "I brought the *fantasy*."

"The what?" asked Erik.

"The *drama*."

"Huh?"

"You'll see."

Allie walked in with something that looked like it was part electric guitar, part jet engine, and part pasta maker.

"Begin.Transmission . . . Conversation. Mode. Activated . . . Are.You.Dudes.Ready.Question. Mark . . . Continue.Transmission."

"Whoaaaaa," Erik said swooningly. "What is that thing?"

"This.Device.Is.Designated.The.Sonic. Explodinator."

Vlad pointed at the thick wires along the neck. "What's this part?"

"That.Is.Designated.The.Tonal.Selector."

Erik leaned in toward the large cone. "What does this do?"

"That.Is.Designated.The.Sonic.Booster."

Vlad gestured at the pasta maker–looking part. "And this?"

Allie pressed a button, and several little tan strings oozed out. "That.Is.Designated. The.Carbo.Filament.Squirter . . . The.Carbo.

Filament.Squirter.Dispenses.Energy . . . End.
Transmission."

Erik plucked a noodle and popped it into his mouth. "Oh, so it *is* a pasta maker. Neat. Anyway, I'll be playing the keyboard. And I guess Vlad is—"

"I'm the singer and creative director. Now, let's talk about our band's name. I have a list of excellent options." Vlad opened his suitcase slightly and pulled out two sheets of paper. He handed them to Allie. "Allie, would you please take one and pass the rest around?"

Allie handed Erik a sheet of paper.

"Let's see," said Erik. "'Vlad and the Nightmares. Vlad and the Maggots. Vlad's Lads. Vlad and the'—these all have your name in them."

"The fans need to be able to cling to someone out front. A lead singer. A focal point." Vlad walked back and forth in the garage, blowing kisses to a future crowd. "It's just for show. We're all equal partners here."

"Begin.Transmission . . . This.Being.Agrees. To.Said.Terms . . . End.Transmission."

"Great," said Vlad. "So, let's go with Vlad and the Maggots. Now for our look." Vlad pulled two paper bags from his suitcase and handed them to Erik. "Would you please pass these out? Thank you."

Erik handed Allie one of the paper bags.

The bags contained antennae headbands and long yellow gowns. Allie twitched for a moment. "Begin.Transmission . . . Error. Detected . . . Maggots.Do.Not.Possess. Antennae . . . End.Transmission."

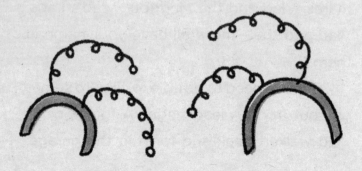

Vlad threw his hands up in frustration. "*Please* trust my artistic vision." Vlad pulled a blood-red cloak from the suitcase, carefully unfolded it, and tied it around his shoulders. He examined the edges and plucked a tiny piece of lint from the velvet.

"I feel like we can come back to this later," said Erik. "We should probably spend, I'd say, *most* of our time on the music. Do you want to hear one of the songs I wrote? I can play it, and then we can all practice it together. Yeah?"

Allie and Vlad nodded. Erik sat on the ground in front of his keyboard and

Alone in the attic
The darkness calls my name
Spiders crawl across my face
I'll never be the same

Without you
Without you
Without you
Without you.

sheet music, took a deep breath, and played a thick, dismal chord. He held it for a few seconds . . . and sang.

"Erik," interrupted Vlad. "Sorry to cut you off. I'm just so inspired."

"You like it?"

"I love it, buddy. I really do. Great stuff. It's just . . ."

"What is it?"

"It just doesn't have that Vlad and the Maggots *edge* people have come to expect. May I?" Vlad took the sheet music and pulled a red pen out of his shirt pocket. "Okay, right here at the beginning. 'Alone in the attic.' That's so sad. I don't want to be alone in an attic. I want to be at a party with tons of fans." Vlad circled the offending line and scribbled *make more epic* above it. Vlad scanned the page. "Spiders, that's good . . . ah, this. 'I'll never be the same without you, without you, without'—it's just *bleaaaugh*. Songs are supposed to be about fun and revenge and skating where you're not supposed to skate. There are seven verses in this song, and you never mention skating. Not even once."

Vlad crossed out verses three through seven and wrote *make more dangerous.*

Erik snatched the paper from Vlad's hands. "These lyrics are from my *soul.* I'm not okay with you changing them."

"Erik. It's not just the lyrics. Allie—back me up here."

"Begin.Transmission . . . This.Being. Desires.Louder.And.Faster.Audio . . . Crank. It.Maggots . . . End.Transmission."

Vlad punched the air. "You heard 'em. Let's *wail.*"

FWOOOOOOM! Allie's Sonic Explodinator blasted a low, deep note that knocked Erik and Vlad against the wall. The power went out in the garage. A car alarm blared in the distance.

Vlad stomped out the fire that had engulfed Erik's

sheet music. "Yes! *That* is what the fans are asking for."

Erik stood up, gathered the charred scraps of his songs, picked up his keyboard, and went inside the house. Vlad and the Maggots was finished.

When Erik got to school the next morning, he saw Allie standing alone on the playground. She was staring at a big rock. Erik walked over and stood next to her.

"Wow," said Erik. "This is where it all started."

Vlad glided up next to them. "Hey, guys. Check this out."

Vlad unfolded a piece of paper. It was a drawing of their three heads and read

VLAD AND THE MAGGOTS across the top. "Those were some great times," he said.

Allie nodded. "Begin.Transmission . . . Agreed . . . Conversation.Mode.Activated . . . Continue.Transmission."

Erik looked at Vlad, then at Allie. "I'm playing Emma's party as a solo act, but maybe we can have a reunion someday. If you want. I know the fans would love it."

"Vlad and the Maggots forever," said Vlad.

"Vlad and the Maggots forever," said Erik.

"Vlad.And.The.Maggots.Forever . . . End. Transmission," said Allie.

BOBBY: SAUCEOLOGIST

After years of intense study, I have concluded that any two foods, no matter how unrelated, can be enjoyed together by employing a "sauce bridge."

This chart will demonstrate a small *taste* (ahem) of my thesis in action.

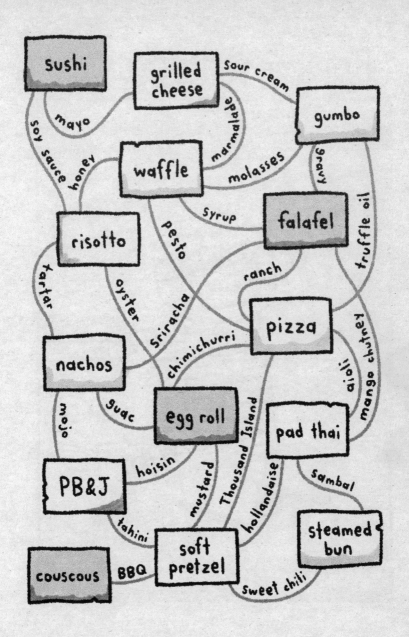

EMMA'S NEW CLOTHES

Emma always wore the same plain white wraps from head to toe. She loved her wraps. They were cozy and simple, and they kept her rotting body from falling apart most of the time. She never considered changing things up.

But the morning before Emma's birthday party/coronation as god-queen of her family's currently nonexistent empire, her mummy came in and said, "This will not do at all. Emma, we're going to get you a new outfit for your coronation tomorrow."

Emma looked down at her plain white wraps. They were soft and kinda stretchy and felt like a full-body hug. Linen is a very breathable fabric, you know. Natural. Absorbent. Holds your bones together.

"And while we're at the mall," added Emma's mummy, "we can get egg rolls."

Emma's eyes lit up. "Eeeeeeggggggggggg rooooollllllllllsss," she groaned. "Yuuummm."*

---

* WHY DID EMMA LOVE EGG ROLLS SO MUCH? LET'S SEE. AN EGG ROLL IS A BUNCH OF SHREDDED-UP BITS OF ASSORTED STUFF SECURED BY A COZY AND SIMPLE WRAP. YEP.

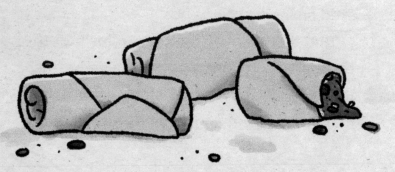

The mall on Creep's Cove is a lot like any shopping center that you've been to. Clothing stores, gift shops, a fountain haunted by dozens of screaming water spirits, a food court, and a department store with electronics, housewares, and cursed talismans.

At Freeq Kids, Emma's mummy pulled item after item out of the heaps. Pink dresses and yellow shirts and orange shorts and blue vests. Striped rompers and plaid skirts and polka-dotted socks. But Emma

didn't like anything more than her cozy and simple plain white wraps.

"Oh, Emma," said Emma's mummy. "If you would just pick something out, we can go get egg rolls."

Emma quickly pointed at a black dress with a red bow. "Eeeeeeeeeggggggggggggg rooooolllllllllsss," she groaned. "Yuuuummm-mmm."

Emma's mummy paid for the dress with a chunky gold coin and was immediately dragged by her daughter across the mall to Mogwai's Wok.

"WHAT? WHAT COULD YOU POSSI-BLY EVEN WANT FROM ME?!" snarled the gremlin behind the counter.

"Eeeeeeeeeggggggggggg rooooolllllllllsss," moaned Emma.

"HOW MANY, YOU STUMBLING BAG OF PRUNES?!"

"Hi, Nuan," said Emma's mummy. "We'll take a demon's dozen." **"YEP. YOU GOT IT, MADAME NEFERMETUM."** Nuan chucked eleven egg rolls into a bag one by one. **"NOW BEAT IT!"**

When she woke up the next morning, Emma looked at her new dress and frowned. It wasn't her, and it wasn't worth the egg rolls. Just then, Emma's mummy called to her from the living room. "Emma! Come see the decorations."

Emma walked into the living room to find a banner, games, a table set up with pyramid party hats, and her mummy hanging a gloomy rainbow of colorful streamers

across the room.
Black, silver, blue, red,
green, and gold.
"Wooooowwwwww,"
groaned Emma.
Her eyes grew
as wide as eggs.
One of them fell
out.

Emma reached out
and draped a green
streamer over her arm.
Emma's mummy looked down and smiled.
"I think it's time to put on your new birthday outfit."

Soon the house was full of all of Emma's
friends, excited to celebrate her coronation
(whatever that was). Emma stood proudly
in the center of the room, holding court
in her brand-new, cozy and colorful, very-
very-Emma, not-so-simple wraps.

Just a bit on the cheeks, please. My personality should be the only thing shining on camera.

TERRIBLE TOPICS:

TELL US ABOUT YOUR

PARENTS

My moms destroyed like ten cities. But I get in trouble for breaking a couple flowerpots?

They're hippo pits!

Hypocrites.

YAAAAAA!!!

Ooh, and blueberries. And strawberries. All berries, really.

I mean... my dad *thinks* he's the alpha.

I wrote a song about them.

♪ FATHER! ♪

I haven't seen my
parents in years.

Get it?

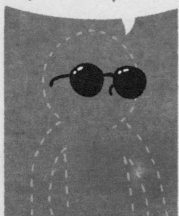

Bobby! Mom says
you gotta glorf
me home.

Fiiine. Let's go.

BOBBY'S FEAST

Bobby stayed up way too late watching the T.U.F.F. Squad™ movie marathon and slept through breakfast. When he woke up and saw that Emma's party was only three hours away, he made a decision.

You see, if there was one thing Bobby flarfed, it was that sequels are always better than the original.*And if there was a *second* thing Bobby flarbed, it was that fancy parties always have the best food. And *this* party was at Emma's house, one of the biggest, fanciest houses on the island. Her mom was some sort of queen, or deity, or both, so he knew she'd come through with some serious grub. Bobby decided to not chibble anything until the party, and then . . . he would *bliff.*

Bobby slorbbed downstairs and kobbed a whiff of pancakes. *Nonono,* he noffed to himself. *Remember the bliff.*

---

* T.U.F.F. SQUAD™ MOVIES, RANKED FROM BEST TO WORST: (1) T.U.F.F. SQUAD™ IN SPACE; (2) T.U.F.F. SQUAD™ GOES WEST; (3) T.U.F.F. SQUAD™: THE TUFFENING; (4) 2 T.U.F.F. 2 FABULOUS; (5) T.U.F.F. SQUAD™ 3D; (6) T.U.F.F. SQUAD™: BEARD CONTEST; (7) THE T.U.F.F.E.S.T; (8) T.U.F.F. SQUAD™ VS. THE BIG PILE OF DIRT; (9) A VERY SPECIAL T.U.F.F. SQUAD™ BIRTHDAY ADVENTURE; (10) ARE YOU T.U.F.F. ENUFF?; (11) T.U.F.F. SQUAD™ TOO; (12) T.U.F.F. 4 LIFE; (13) T.U.F.F. SQUAD™

Bobby's mom torbled around the corner. "We've still got some pancakes, kiddo!" she plurfed. "We've got onions! We've got candy corn! We've got sardines!"

"Moooooom," glirped Robbi, Bobby's sister. "We're out of syyyrup."

"Switch to gravy," flupped Bobby's mom.

"Hooray!"

All of that delicious food jaffle was too much for Bobby, so he floofed back up-stairs, away from temptation.

Finally, it was time to horf on over to Emma's house. He snorbled out the back door to avoid his sister's plebbling to plob along. He duppled under his breath as he blurped down the street. *Dips and cakes and*

fiiinger foods. Dips and cakes and fiiinger foods.

The front door was open, so Bobby slurbbed in and goo-lined it over to the snack altar. It was just as he'd imagined it. Dips, ✓. Cakes, ✓. Finger foods, ✓✓✓. *Let's see,* he thought. *First, some light chip-dipping. Then those slugs-in-a-blanket, then—*

"I demand everyone's complete attention," boomed a voice. It was Emma's
mummy, dressed in a flowing black gown
and dripping with gold and jewels.

"Come on, Bobby," said Quade. "It's time
for the ceremony. Here." Quade placed a
pyramid-shaped party hat on Bobby and

led him over to the base of a small set of steps.

"Behold," said Emma's mummy. "I, Queen Nefermetum of the Immortal Dynasty of Nefermetum, have ruled my empire in exile for five thousand years. The time has come for the coronation of my dear daughter Emmagowaybak. One day she will take back what is ours and lay waste to the world of humans."[*]

The speech went on for several more minutes. Bobby couldn't fleef his eyes off the snack altar. When Emma's mummy said, "Now tremble in fear and have some

---

[*] THE GROWN-UPS ON CREEP'S COVE HAVE DOZENS OF PROPHE-CIES AND VISIONS AND GOALS FOR THEIR KIDS ABOUT ALL SORTS OF REVENGE AND WORLD DOMINATION. THEY CAN'T AGREE ON WHICH VERSION THEY SHOULD ALL GO WITH, SO YOU SHOULDN'T WORRY ABOUT IT HAPPENING ANYTIME SOON.

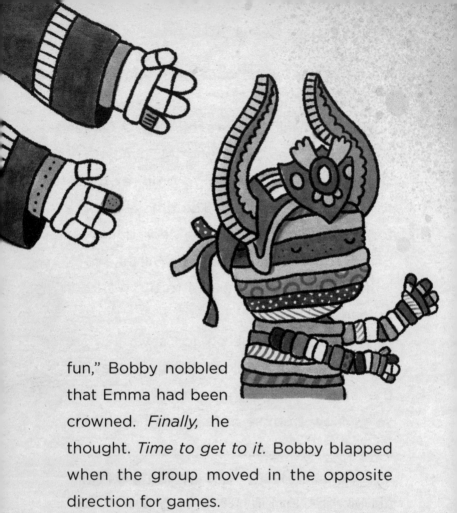

fun," Bobby nobbled
that Emma had been
crowned. *Finally*, he
thought. *Time to get to it.* Bobby blapped
when the group moved in the opposite
direction for games.

There was a large drawing of a black
horse on the wall and a stack of cutout
horns and pushpins on the ground next to
it. "Great," thubbed Bobby. "Pin the Horns

on the Tredicorn. Surely we don't have to get all *thirteen* horns on the thing."

"... and the game isn't over until all thirteen horns are pinned on the tredicorn," said Emma's mummy. Bobby slurfed in agony. The kids stood around the would-be tredicorn. Each took a turn being blindfolded and spun around before attempting to put a horn in just the right spot. Emma missed, Vlad missed, Griff missed. Lizzie missed but also somehow managed to stab herself in the tail. It wasn't until the second time around that Allie got the first horn in place.

Bobby's whole body hurgled with hunger. "Okay, this is ridiculous." He murped over to the pair of floating sunglasses across from him. "Psst! Griff! Want to help move this game along?"

"You know . . . ," said Griff. "Unicorn, sure. Bicorn, no problem. Tricorn, why not? Quadricorn, okay. Pentahorn, maybe. Hexahorn, hold on. Hepticorn—"

"*Griff!*" schmiggled Bobby.

"But *tredicorn*? That's too far. Yeah, let's wrap this up."

Griff dropped his sunglasses and crept over to a blindfolded Gilly. "Hey," he whispered. "It's me, chumarino. Lemme give you a hand." Gilly's hand swooped across the drawing and perfectly pinned the second horn behind the tredicorn's ear. The kids cheered.

Bobby plipped the third horn on the tredicorn's nose. Frankie pinned the fourth one under its chin. Quade said, "No thanks," and pinned a horn a foot away from the creature's mane. The horn popped off the wall and tacked back down at the base of the tredicorn's neck. The kids jumped up and down and got louder with each horn placement. When Emma pinned horn number thirteen on the tredicorn's heart, the whole group went completely bonkers. Lobo jumped up on a chair and howled. Lizzie ripped the tredicorn off the wall and tore it to shreds. Griff, feeling like the ultimate champion of Pin the Horns on the Tredicorn, danced around the room with such precision and passion that he immediately would have been offered scholarships to all the top dance academies in the world . . . if anyone on earth had seen it. Bobby flammed straight to the snack altar.

Casual, polite chip-dipping wasn't going to cut it. Bobby rulfed the entire bowl of dip in one splurf. The slugs-in-a-blanket went in three at a time and were followed by a train of egg rolls. The room was spinning. Then . . . a distant voice. Slowly, Lizzie came into focus.

"You're eating the table, weirdo!" *What?* Bobby larfed down, and sure enough, half of the altar was in his body. He tried to hurf it out, but it only marfed deeper into his side.

Emma's mummy came around the corner. "Bobby, dear, I just got off the phone with your mom. She told me to make sure you don't eat any of the dip. Cauliflower makes your tummy a little bloated.* Oh . . ."

Bobby's whole *Bobby* gorfled and expanded. The rest of the snack altar was in him now, as well as a nearby chair. He was out of control.

The stack of presents was next. In they went. Then the couch, including Allie, who was sitting on it. She waved at Frankie through the ooze. The kids backed against the wall, screaming and trying to get away. "Bobby!" shouted Lizzie. "Don't you **DARE** absorb any more of us."

"I'm . . . trying," snurfed Bobby. But there

---

* CAULIFLOWER IS IN THE *BRASSICA* GENUS AND IS RELATED TO BROCCOLI, BRUSSELS SPROUTS, CABBAGE, ETC. THESE FOODS CAN HAVE A CERTAIN . . . EFFECT ON SOME PEOPLE.

was no stopping him. The expanding goo filled and engulfed the entire house from the inside out.

With her top half still outside her friend,

Frankie grabbed her phone and made a call. "Adam. Has a ship come in this afternoon? Still docked? What's on it? Okay . . . okay . . . okay . . . **AHA!** Expect a pickup in a few minutes."

Frankie tossed Lizzie her phone. "Call your mom. The flying one."

Bobby had graffled to the neighboring houses in every direction. Cars, trees, a group of gnome tourists—they were all inside the gelatinous glob. A dark shadow passed overhead. Those who could still move looked up and saw Lizzie's mom soaring above them, clutching a shipping container in her murderous claws.

The front door of the container opened, and a shower of cabbage and broccoli poured out. When Bobby's body plaffed the vegetables, he stopped darlfling out and baffed just in that direction. "More!" shouted Frankie. "So much more!"

Lizzie's mom circled back and poured more vegetables halfway up the block. Bobby blorbled the food, nurbling more and more. "This seems like the exact *opposite* of what we should be doing!" yelled Vlad through the growing glop.

"Trust me," called Frankie. "He has to be *huge.*" She turned back toward Bobby's face. "Just concentrate on not digesting us, chumarino!"

My catchphrase is "a thing"! thought Griff. *Best Satur-hang ever!*

Lizzie's mom continued to drop a stream of cabbage and broccoli on the street toward the center of the island. As the massive, full-of-everything glob flibbled uphill toward the mouth of the volcano, the monsters whose faces were sticking out of the goo cried out in abject horror.

The last of the vegetables were dropped

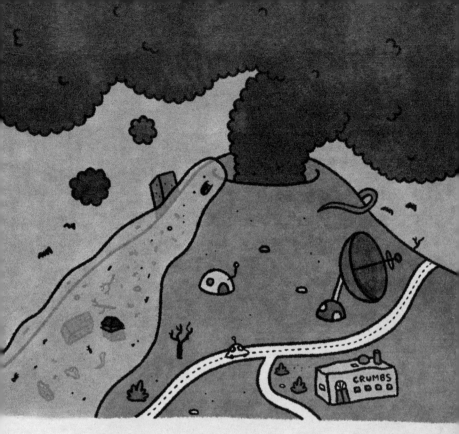

into the bubbling mouth of Creep's Cove's
heart. Bobby sworfed toward it. "Come
on . . . ," said Frankie. "It's not enough to go
in. . . . He needs to . . . Yes!"

The front of the great goo worm that was
Bobby glipped the mouth of the volcano

and began to pliffle like a balloon. Frankie
held her breath and crossed her fingers as
she sank into her pink translucent tomb.

The explosion rang out across the island. The cars, the creatures, the houses,
the stuff, and chunks of Bobby were

frupped in every direction. Quade landed
near Allie and helped her up. Lizzie roared,
"Call the fire brigade! Call the mayor! Call
my lawyer!" from a treetop. The family of
gnome tourists wiped the Bobby from their
faces and decided to cut their vacation
short.

Frankie stumbled around the wreckage
until she found a small pink dollop with a

face. She carefully picked it up and tapped it on the cheek. "Bobby? Still with us?"

Bobby snorfed and worgled like a little baby nugget. "I couldn't help it, Frankie. I'm so . . . so sorry."

Frankie looked around to make sure no

one was listening. "It's okay, Bobby," she said. "Cruciferous veggies make me a little gassy, too."

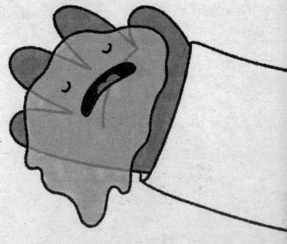

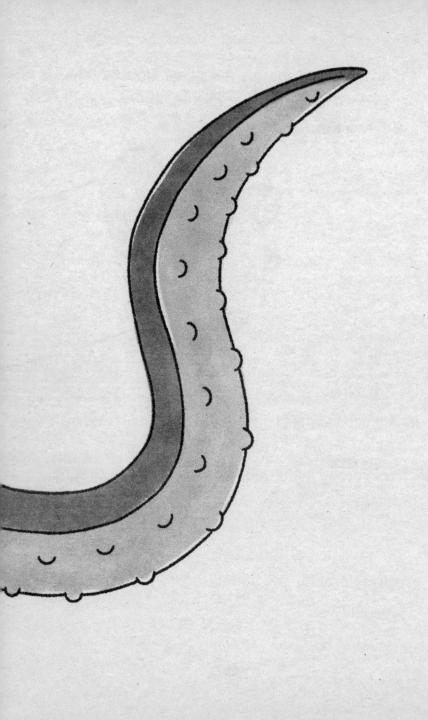

MS. VERNE'S LESSON

There are few joys greater than walking into your classroom and finding out it's movie day. That's something that all kids, whether human, monster, ghost, alien, or otherwise, have in common.

So when the kids of the older-ish class at Stubtoe Elementary saw "the ol' telly-welly," as Griff called it and was hoping to make into "a thing," they whisper-cheered and ferociously debated what they'd be watching.

"I hope we're watching *The Most Ghosts*," said Vlad.

"No way," snorted Lobo. "It has to be educational."

"Excuse me, but *The Most Ghosts* is very, *very* educational," said Vlad. "*Most* is a number: that's math. *Ghosts:* that's paranormal biology."

"Okay, you got me there."

"I bet it's just a bunch of boring stuff from Ms. Verne's boring vacation to the boring center of the boring earth," groaned Lizzie. "This is the worst day of my life."

WELL, I STALAG-MIGHT.

"Nay," said Gilly.

"Nay what?" asked Erik. "What do you think we're watching?"

"Oh, I haven't a hunch," said Gilly. "Just nay."

Ms. Verne whooshed in and whacked a tentacle against the wall to get the class's attention. "¶Σ2°Δ˙ ∂°Δ˙∂Σœi£≤."

Quade got up and turned off the lights.

"∫∂̊°Δ∂∫œª´›¬ss," said Ms. Verne. "¿Δ∞∂∂̊ °∫≤µ˜∂̊°≠ ∂æΩ. ∏œss Σ˙ss≤∫Ó ï Î°‰˜ı∏!"

"Cool," said Frankie.

"Um, yeah," said Erik. "Cool."

"Let's get this shibbidy-shoo on the razzle," said Griff.

Ms. Verne smacked the PLAY button.

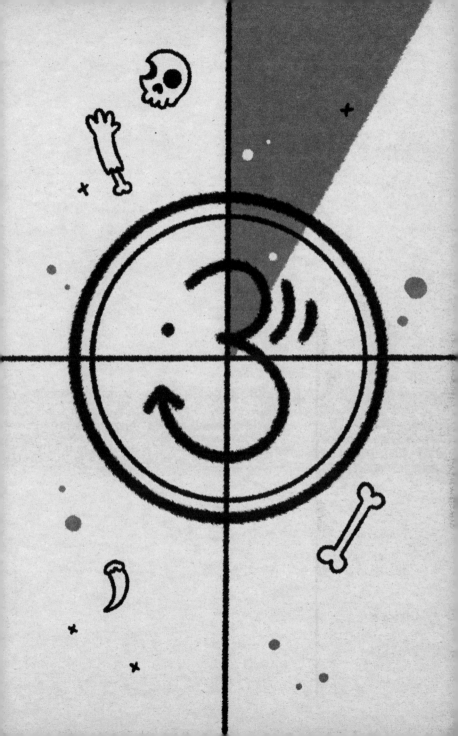

The DANGEROUS WORLD of HüMAN BEINGS

Hey, dummies. I'm "Dr." Stoker, and I've been studying human beings for, like, a while.

I'm here to tell YOU all about them. So listen to me. Now.

Check this out. That sauce is made from the hottest peppers on earth. He's crying and sweating from it.

CHAPTER 1: FOOD

But LOOK. He's going back for MORE! What?!

And how 'bout this? This lady has a drink that's so cold it's FREEZING HER BRAIN. Then...

ANOTHER SIP?! HOW?!

Humans are scared of our kind.
That's a fact. But behold this
with your faces. BEHOLD.

CHAPTER 2: ENTERTAINMENT

They make movies about us...
and watch them for FUN.

And LOOK. Some humans jump out of airplanes... for FUN.

And some of them draw pictures on their bodies with NEEDLES.

Look at THESE humans.

They're exposing themselves to the sun's radiation. On PURPOSE.

Human beings are everywhere. Visit the most teeth-chatteringly cold spots, and they're there.

CHAPTER 3: HOME LIFE

Go to the most miserably hot places on Earth—tons of humans.

When their settlements are destroyed, they rebuild them... in the same exact place.

They MOCK NATURE.

They captured some of the fiercest animals around—*wild dogs*—and slowly...patiently...

...turned them into their furry little friends. Terrifying!

"Begin.Transmission... That.Was.Chilling...
End.Transmission," said Allie.

"SCAAAAAAARRRRRRRYYY," groaned
Emma.

"I don't want to do tricks for treats," said Lobo. "I just want treats for being a good boy."

"You are a good boy, Lobo," said Frankie. "You're such a good boy. Here." Frankie tossed Lobo a cookie.

"This changes everything," said Lizzie. "I always assumed we'd grow up, head to the mainland, and take over, like the old days. But humans are terrifying. No offense, Frankie. Some offense, Erik."

"Yeah, none taken," said Frankie. "I'm with you. We should just stay here where it's safe."

"Definitely," flurbed Bobby.

The kids were quiet. Their minds raced and churned with the horrors that they had just witnessed and the uncertainty of the future. Everything felt scary and big. It was Vlad who broke the silence.

"Hey! A meteorite crashed in my back-
yard last night, and there's a bunch of glowing gunk coming out of it. Who wants to
come over after school, dip stuff in it, and
see what happens?"

Everything suddenly felt a little more
normal again.

for now. Keep your eyeballs peeled for **The Terribles** in their next collection of tales:

A WITCH'S LAST RESORT

GLOB TALK

A GUIDE TO BOBBY'S VERBS

TALK, SAY, ASK, WONDER, OR YELL

blurf	jaffle
flup	jorgle
flurb	noff
glirp	plurf
glurf	porf
glurm	schmiggle
gorgle	snurf
gurfle	thub

MOVE, SPREAD, EXIT, OR ESCAPE

baff	blurp
blorble	dorble

durf

flam

flibble

floof

florb

glop

gorfle

horf

lorf

marf

murp

plob

slorb

slurb

torble

EAT

bliff

chibble

rulf

STRETCH, EXPAND

darlfling

graffle

nurble

skwibble

splarg

sworf

MIXED BAG

blap—**GROAN**

diffle—**SHUT**

dupple—**SING**

flarb—**UNDERSTAND, KNOW**

flarf—**UNDERSTAND, KNOW**

fleef—**KEEP**

flurf—**ABSORB**

frup—**THROW, BLAST**

glip—**COVER**

gloof—**HIDE**

glorf—**ACCOMPANY**

glorp—**ABSORB**

hurf—**PUSH (IT)**

hurgle—**QUIVER**

klof—**SMACK, PUSH**

kob—**CATCH**

larf—**LOOK**

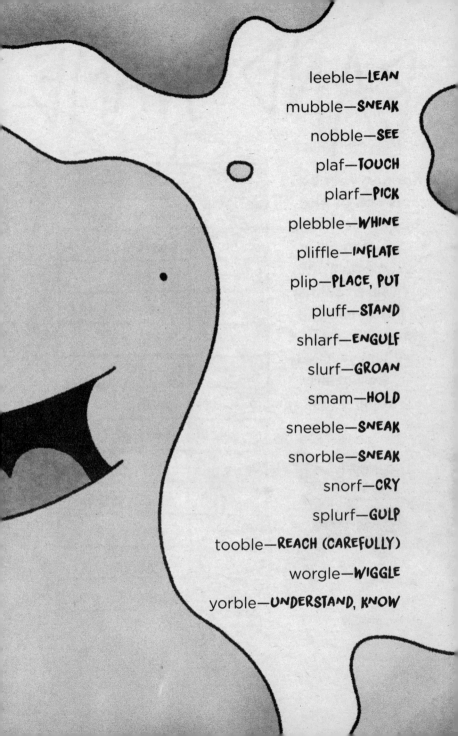

leeble—**LEAN**

mubble—**SNEAK**

nobble—**SEE**

plaf—**TOUCH**

plarf—**PICK**

plebble—**WHINE**

pliffle—**INFLATE**

plip—**PLACE, PUT**

pluff—**STAND**

shlarf—**ENGULF**

slurf—**GROAN**

smam—**HOLD**

sneeble—**SNEAK**

snorble—**SNEAK**

snorf—**CRY**

splurf—**GULP**

tooble—**REACH (CAREFULLY)**

worgle—**WIGGLE**

yorble—**UNDERSTAND, KNOW**

BAND NAME

Naming your band is one of the biggest decisions you'll make in your entire life. If you're feeling stuck, use this tool, and you'll be well on your way to world domination.

First letter of ur name	
A or B	Corn Chips
C or D	Daisy
E or F	Brick
G or H	Clown Shoes
I or J	Pickle
K or L	Boogers
M or N	Chilly
O or P	Spike
Q or R	Bat Face
S or T	Shoe String
U or V	Candace
W or X	Pumpkin Girl
Y or Z	Waffles

GENERATOR

2 ⟶ 3

BIRTH MONTH (OPTIONAL)	
Jan	& the
Feb	with
Mar	but not
Apr	says
May	without
Jun	& the
Jul	with
Aug	but not
Sep	says
Oct	without
Nov	loves
Dec	& the

Favorite color	
Red	Juice Box
Orange	Cheesies
Yellow	Nothingness
Green	Daydreams
Blue	Guts
Purple	Silliness
Pink	Night Terrors
Black	Extra Sauce
Brown	Breadsticks
White	Quicksand
Gray	Chaos
Stripes	Let's Go!
Plaid	Lil' Babies

Not liking what you generated?
Change it. NO RULES! EVER!

YEARLING HUMOR!

Looking for more funny books to read?
Check these out!

- ❏ *Bad Girls* by Jacqueline Wilson
- ❏ Calvin Coconut: *Trouble Magnet* by Graham Salisbury
- ❏ *Don't Make Me Smile* by Barbara Park
- ❏ *Fern Verdant and the Silver Rose* by Diana Leszczynski
- ❏ *Funny Frank* by Dick King-Smith
- ❏ *Gooney Bird Greene* by Lois Lowry
- ❏ *How Tía Lola Came to ~~Visit~~ Stay* by Julia Alvarez
- ❏ *How to Save Your Tail* by Mary Hanson
- ❏ *I Was a Third Grade Science Project* by Mary Jane Auch

- ❏ *Jelly Belly* by Robert Kimmel Smith
- ❏ *Lawn Boy* by Gary Paulsen
- ❏ *Nim's Island* by Wendy Orr
- ❏ *Out of Patience* by Brian Meehl
- ❏ Shredderman: *Secret Identity* by Wendelin Van Draanen
- ❏ *Toad Rage* by Morris Gleitzman
- ❏ *A Traitor Among the Boys* by Phyllis Reynolds Naylor